The New Adventures of F

t

Postman Pat

and the Beast of Greendale

John Cunliffe
Illustrated by Stuart Trotter

from the original television designs by **Ivor Wood**

Hodder
Children's
Books

a division of Hodder Headline plc

More Postman Pat adventures:

Postman Pat and the mystery tour
Postman Pat and the robot
Postman Pat takes flight
Postman Pat and the big surprise
Postman Pat paints the ceiling
Postman Pat has too many parcels
Postman Pat and the suit of armour
Postman Pat and the hole in the road
Postman Pat has the best village
Postman Pat misses the show
Postman Pat follows a trail
Postman Pat in a muddle

First published in 1998
by Hodder Children's Books,
a division of Hodder Headline plc
338 Euston Road, London NW1 3BH

ISBN 0 340 67816 X   (HB)
ISBN 0 340 71332 1   (PB)
10 9 8 7 6 5 4 3 2 1

Printed in Italy.

It had been a quiet morning in Greendale - until Pat came walking fast round a corner, and sent Miss Hubbard's bike flying!

What a hurry he was in! He didn't stop for a chat or a cup of tea anywhere, today. He did stop in his tracks, though, when he came out of Greendale Farm and saw Jess perched on the roof of the van, with his fur bristling.

"Hey up, Jess, what's happened?" said Pat.

The door was open, and Pat's sandwich-box was lying on the ground.

"Oh, my sandwiches!" Pat moaned. "Who's done that? Rotten lot! They've eaten every last one! The sandwich-robbers of Greendale strike again! It can't be the hens this time . . . We'd better be off, Jess."

Pat was on his way.

"You never know . . ." he said to Jess,
". . . they might start cat-napping cats, next!"

But Jess wasn't listening. He was having
a cat-nap. All this rushing about was too
much for him!

At Thompson Ground, Pat called out, "Morning, Dorothy! Lots of letters for you today!"

"Thanks, Pat! Any news?"

"There's news alright! Someone's pinched my lunch, while I was parked at Greendale Farm. Terrified poor old Jess, as well!"

"Oh, dear," said Dorothy, "who could have done that? But never mind, I have something nice in the oven. There's plenty to spare, so don't you worry."

"Oooh, Dorothy, that sounds grand. You are kind. What a treat!"

"Just come and have a look at my carrots first," said Dorothy.
"They're real champions . . . Oh, heavens! What's happened to them?"
   You never saw such a mess. Someone had tramped and
trampled all over the garden!

"I don't believe it!" said Pat.

"What a monster," wailed Dorothy, "to do a thing like this! Just look at what's left of my lovely carrots!"

"First it was my sandwiches, now it's your carrots," said Pat. "It must be a very hungry monster!"

Dorothy said, "I'm going to ring PC Selby. It might be a dangerous animal, escaped from a circus: a lion - or a tiger. . ."

Poor old Pat! Dorothy was in such a fluster that she had forgotten all about lunch.

Pat and Jess went on their way, feeling more and more hungry, and keeping a look-out for the monster.

There was something going on at Granny Dryden's cottage, too. All the washing had been thrown into the road. Granny Dryden was looking over the wall in great distress.

"Oh, Pat! Look at my washing! The line's broken, and my new sheets all dirty in the road, and my best pillow-case has gone!"

"That's only the half of it!" said Pat. "There's been trouble all up the dale . . . Someone pinched my lunch, and made a mess of Dorothy Thompson's prize carrots, and now your washing! It might be a beast from the moors. Best stay safe indoors, till PC Selby catches up with it. Don't worry, now. You'll be alright!"

"Bye, Pat! Mind how you go!"

Jess was wishing that the beast was a nice fat mouse.

He was very hungry, and so was Pat.

Later, they came upon Miss Hubbard's bike at the road-side, fallen in the ditch, with everything spilling out of her basket.

"What now?" said Pat.

Miss Hubbard was hiding behind the wall. She popped up when she heard Pat.

"Oh, Pat! How glad I am to see you!" she gasped.

"What happened?" said Pat. "Have you had an accident?"

"I met the - the - beast - you know - this beast that folks are talking about."

"What sort of beast was it?"

"It had a huge head, all covered in something white. It snorted at me, and stamped its hooves, and snatched two apples out of my basket, then it galloped off."

Pat lifted Miss Hubbard's bike out of the ditch, and gathered up her shopping.

"I'll tell PC Selby as soon as I get to the village," he said. "Will you be OK now?"

"Oh, yes, I'll be fine; thanks, Pat. You'd better get on with your letters. Mind how you go!"

"Cheerio!"

Pat went on his way. He had a registered letter for Major Forbes.
When they arrived at Garner Hall, the Major was busy in the garden.

"Morning!" said Pat, "there's a special letter for you . . ."

"Look at this, Pat!" said the Major. "My best begonias; squashed flat! I spotted it myself! A huge monster, rampaging all round the garden, with a mysterious white shroud over its head!"

"Bless me, Major," said Pat. "I never saw such a mess in all my days! I do hear that it's the famous Beast of Greendale, risen from its lair in the moors . . ."

"Bah! I'll give it Beast of Greendale, making a mess of my garden. We'll have to hunt the thing down - chase it back to the moors . . ."

"Listen!" said Pat, holding his hand to his ear.

"Bells?" said the Major. "I haven't missed the bell-ringing practice, have I?"

"No, Major, that's on Tuesday," said Pat. "No, I think the Reverend must be ringing them."

"Calling for help!" shouted the Major. "Perhaps that Beast's after him. Come on, Pat, we'll take the short-cut - not a minute to lose!"

Major Forbes led the way; across a field, through some very prickly bushes, and a few quite muddy puddles. They found the Reverend Timms in the church-yard, looking very upset about something.

"Hello, Reverend! Anything wrong?"

"Oh, Major . . . and Pat . . ." said the Reverend. "I am glad you've come. . ."

"Did you ring the bells for help?" said Pat.

"No, I didn't ring them at all! I don't know who did!"

"Right, men," said Major Forbes. "We'd better investigate! No need to be scared."

"Lead the way, Major!" said Pat.

"Er - well - I think you should go first, Pat - I'll bring up the rear - back you up, you know - reinforcements, we call it in the army - in you go, Pat!"

Pat pushed the door open, and peeped inside.

"Anybody there?"

There was no answer, so Pat went softly into the church. There was a sound of bumping and banging and stamping; something snorting; someone having a struggle . . .

"What can you see?" said the Reverend, following at a safe distance.

"Well . . . I'm not sure," said Pat. "Are you coming?"

"Well - no - bad strategy . . . " said Major Forbes, keeping well back.

"We'll stay here - secure your line of retreat - forward, Pat, forward - don't be scared!"

They hid behind a pew, whilst Pat crept along the length of the church. Another door was partly open, and the noises seemed to be coming from behind it. Pat put his head round it to see what was going on.

"Ooooh, errrrrrrr!!!" he yelled, shutting the door with a bang. "I think we've found it - the - the - beast!" he said. "Come and have a look."

"Bless us all, Pat, what can it be?" said the Reverend Timms, creeping up to the door behind Pat.

Pat opened the door a little way, so that they could all peep through the gap. There, they saw an amazing sight. PC Selby was fighting the beast. He had thrown a pillow-case over its head, and he was trying to push it out of the church. The bell-rope had become tangled round them, so that the bell clanged away up in the tower.

"You little demon . . . !" gasped PC Selby, pushing with all his might. The pillow-case slipped off the beast's head, and the battle turned into a tug-of-war. Suddenly, the beast let go, sending PC Selby staggering.

The beast galloped into the church-yard, with PC Selby, Pat, the Reverend Timms, and the Major after it. They all dashed round the corner of the tower, and stopped. They could see the animal properly now.

"That's no beast!" said Pat. "It's young Lucy's pony!"

And there was little Lucy Selby, feeding an apple to the Beast of Greendale, and the 'beast' standing quietly whilst she stroked its mane.

"What a naughty girl she's been!" said Lucy.

"Aye, well - it's a pity it took me so long to catch her," said PC Selby. "All the bother she's caused . . ."

"We all thought it was the Beast of Greendale!" said Pat.

"Beast of what?" said PC Selby. "Oh, dear me, it's no beast! It's only Lucy's pony! But I'll make up for any damage it's done, the little devil!"

"I think you'll have a few gardens to dig and put to rights," said Pat.

"I'll help!" said Lucy.

"We'll all help!" said the Reverend.

"Beast of Greendale, indeed!" said the Major. "Not much of a beast! Didn't scare me; not for a minute!"

"Bless her!" murmured the Reverend. "She's a lovely pony, really. Just a mischief. Full of fun! I had one like her, when I was a lad . . ."

Lucy was soon ready to ride home.

"Bye bye! Thanks, everybody!" she called.

They all waved to her.

"Bye, Lucy!" said Pat. "Mind how you go!"

"Keep that pony on a tight rein," said PC Selby. "We don't want any more Beast of Greendale adventures."

"*I'd* rather ride home in my van!" said Pat. "For one thing, it doesn't eat carrots or sandwiches!"